STAR WARS

HAN AND THE REBEL RESCUE

ADAPTED BY **NATE MILLICI**

BASED ON **SMUGGLER'S RUN** BY GREG RUCKA

ILLUSTRATED BY **PILOT STUDIO**

Printed in the United States of America
First Paperback Edition, May 2017
1 3 5 7 9 10 8 6 4 2
Library of Congress Control Number on file
FAC-029261-17081
ISBN 978-1-368-00352-0

Visit the official *Star Wars* website at: www.starwars.com.

Disney

LUCASFILM PRESS

LOS ANGELES · NEW YORK

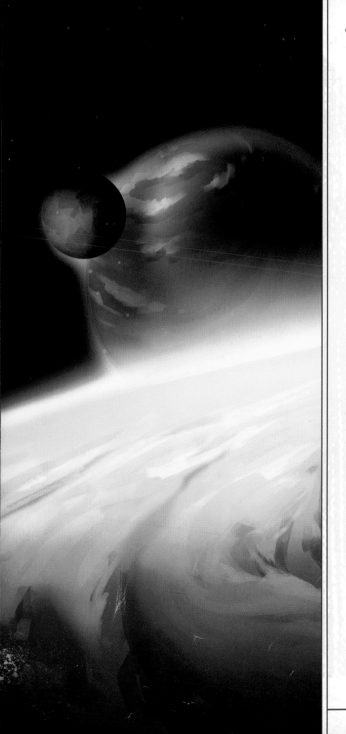

HAN SOLO AND CHEWBACCA WERE ON A SECRET MISSION FOR THE REBELLION.

A rebel spy named Lieutenant Ematt was stranded on a planet called Cyrkon in the Outer Rim. Ematt held top-secret information for the rebels and it was imperative that Han and Chewie find him before the Empire did.

Han had not wanted to help with the mission. He was tired of sticking out his neck for the Rebellion. But Princess Leia knew that only Han and Chewie's ship, the *Millennium Falcon*, was fast enough to reach Cyrkon in time to save Ematt.

Han and Chewie touched down in one of the landing bays and set the engines to standby. Han had a feeling they would need to leave in a hurry.

Before Han and Chewie could even start their search for Ematt, they were surrounded by four bounty hunters!

Han owed money to the vilest gangster in the galaxy, Jabba the Hutt, and the slimy monster had grown impatient for his credits.

Jabba had hired a droid bounty hunter and his three companions to find Han.

Han and Chewie were trapped!

Then, just when Han and Chewie thought things couldn't get worse, a squad of Imperial stormtroopers started marching their way!

But Han had an idea. He shouted at the troopers that the bounty hunters were rebels!

The stormtroopers turned on the bounty hunters, eager to catch any rebel who might be searching for the missing Ematt.

In all the chaos, Han and Chewie managed to slip away unnoticed!

The Wookiee growled in relief.

Han and Chewie weaved their way through the busy marketplace to a cantina where Han knew he could get information about Ematt's location.

But this cantina was unlike any other. It was inside the cargo hold of a ship called the *Miss Fortune*.

    Han greeted a woman with red hair. Her name was Delia, and she owned the
cantina.
    Sure enough, Delia knew exactly where Ematt was hiding. She was surprised
to see Han Solo on a mission for the rebels, but then again, Han was always full
of surprises.

Han and Chewie rented a speeder and raced across the city. They needed to reach Ematt, and fast!

Chewie was not happy about the speeder, though. It had not been designed with Wookiees in mind.

When they reached the hotel where Delia had told them Ematt was hiding,
Han was relieved to find that the rebel was okay.
Ematt was unsure of his rescuers, but there was no time for questions.

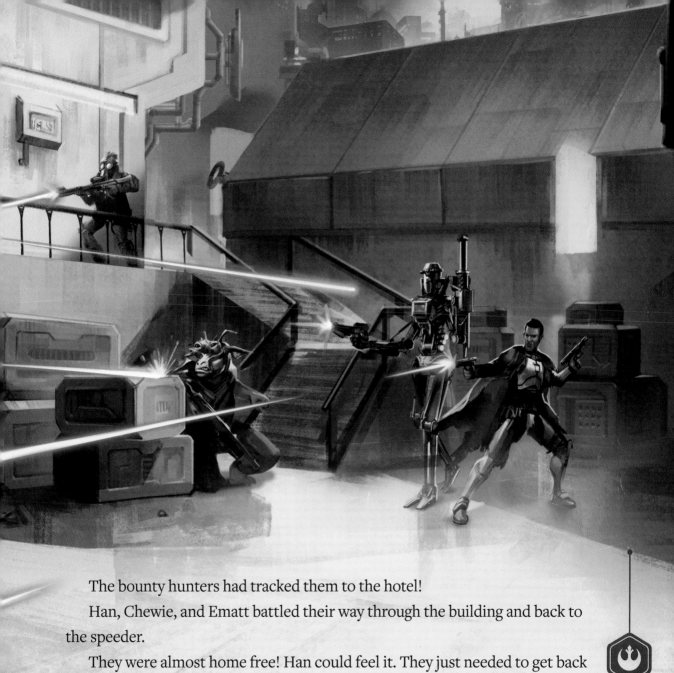

The bounty hunters had tracked them to the hotel!

Han, Chewie, and Ematt battled their way through the building and back to the speeder.

They were almost home free! Han could feel it. They just needed to get back to the *Falcon*.

Of course, nothing ever went quite as planned.

When Han, Chewie, and Ematt reached the landing bay, they ran right into a squad of stormtroopers! The Empire had been waiting for them.

Han's lies had only gotten them so far. The Imperials realized that Chewie and Han, not the bounty hunters, were the *real* rebels. And they were going to take them and Ematt away.

But Han had an idea, and all it took was a wink at Chewie for the Wookiee to catch on.

Chewbacca shoved Han into a pack of stormtroopers. The smuggler flailed, taking down as many troopers as he could.

The diversion worked. Chaos erupted!

Han pulled his blaster and fired at
the generators along the perimeter of
the landing bay. Explosions knocked the
troopers off their feet!

Han noticed a familiar ship lining up a shot from above. It was the *Miss Fortune*!

Delia sent down blasts to keep the troopers at bay while Han, Chewie, and Ematt boarded the *Falcon* and prepared for takeoff. Han had been right: they really *did* need to leave in a hurry.

The *Falcon* roared away from the polluted planet and joined the *Miss Fortune* in space.

An Imperial Star Destroyer was waiting for them, along with a fleet of TIE fighters whizzing this way and that, pelting space with bright green blasts. The Empire was desperate to stop the rebels at any cost!

The Star Destroyer was edging closer, aiming to trap the rebel ships in its tractor beam. Running interference and dodging Imperial blasts, Han and Chewie pushed the *Falcon* to its limits to protect Delia.

After Han saw that the *Miss Fortune* had disappeared into the safety of unknown space, the *Millennium Falcon* jumped to lightspeed—at the last possible second before the Imperial tractor beam could latch on!

Han and Chewie had completed their mission for the Rebellion.
They may have been an unlikely pair of rebels, but they were rebels all the same!